Sand Jewels

G.J. Walker-Smith

Sand Jewels

Print Edition

© 2014 G.J. Walker-Smith

Cover by Scarlett Rugers, http://www.scarlettrugers.com
Formatting by Polgarus Studio, http://www.polgarusstudio.com

Other Books by G.J Walker-Smith
Saving Wishes (Book One, The Wishes Series)
Second Hearts (Book Two, The Wishes Series)
Storm Shells (Book Three, The Wishes Series)
Silver Dawn (Book 4.5, The Wishes Series)
Secret North (Book Four, The Wishes Series)
Star Promise (Book Five, The Wishes Series)

Contact the author:
https://www.facebook.com/gjwalkersmith
gjwalkersmith@gmail.com
gjwalkersmith.com

For everyone who enjoys spending time in La La Land. Thank you for your wonderful support.

CONTENTS

1. BRAT

It was the never-ending day. I checked the time on my watch, sighing at the realisation that it was seven o'clock, and I was still at school.

Parent interviews were not exactly the highlight of my school term. Most of the parents I'd dealt with that night weren't exactly thrilled to be spending time with me either.

I poked my head out the door and looked down the corridor, hopeful of finally making my escape. There was one more person waiting to see me, and I was more than a little surprised to see him.

Alex Blake was the brother and guardian of one of the most insolent, unteachable students I'd ever had.

"Mr Blake," I announced haughtily.

He ambled toward me, grinning smugly. "It's Alex," he corrected. "We're friends, Gabrielle. You buy coffee from me every morning."

"It's Mademoiselle Décarie today," I replied. "This is a formal setting."

Alex walked past me and headed into the empty classroom. "It doesn't look very formal," he noted, glancing around the room.

My heels clicked on the wooden floor as I marched over to my desk and sat down. "It's my workplace."

"You're right." He turned back to face me. "The café is my workplace. Maybe you should call me Mr Blake when ordering your latte."

I frowned across at him. I should've had the upper hand. I'd been waiting to tell him what a disaster his sister was for weeks, but I was having trouble holding my ground.

"Sit down, please," I ordered, pointing to the chair on the other side of my desk.

Alex paced slowly across the room and sat down, keeping his brown eyes locked on mine the whole time. "You didn't come to the café this morning. Why?"

"I was busy."

"I missed seeing you."

I hated his cockiness. The reason he got away with it wasn't complicated. Alex Blake was simply a stunning looking man. I usually favoured well-put together men who put effort into their appearance. My last boyfriend used to spend more time in front of the bathroom mirror than I did. He was perfect, except for the fact that he also used to spend more time in other women's beds than mine.

I wasn't sure Alex even had a bathroom mirror. His floppy sandy hair was in a constant messy state and I'd only seen him clean-shaven a handful of times – and there was something incredibly sexy about it.

He knew the effect he had on me. I'm sure it added to his superior attitude. I'd made it my mission that day to tear him down a peg or two.

"Let's get down to business, shall we?" I asked, shuffling through my notes.

"Yes," he agreed, resting his hands behind his head, "let's."

"Charli failed to submit the last three assignments I gave her," I told him. "She's right on track to fail."

"Does she get credit for being consistent?" he joked.

I slammed the pen I was holding down on my desk. "You're not taking this seriously. She's failing Alex, miserably."

"But she's getting a B in English," he replied, shrugging. "That means she can read and write – pretty competently as it turns out. She's also getting a C in maths. It's not spectacular, but I'll take it. Her competency in French isn't really important to me."

I was furious with him. "A failing grade shouldn't be acceptable in any class!"

He leaned forward, resting his elbows on his knees. "Are you going to cry, Mademoiselle Décarie?"

I straightened up in my seat. "Of course not," I scoffed.

"Good." He smirked at me. "I've just spent twenty-minutes with Mrs Jennings. She has a difficult time teaching Charli too. She was in tears by the end of our meeting," he explained. "The woman teaches cooking. Do you see a pattern forming here?"

"Yes. Your sister is a brat," I hissed.

It was a terrible thing to say. I'd never sunken so low when describing a student, even one as wicked as Charli. I apologised immediately.

"Don't be sorry," he replied, smiling at me. "It's a fair assessment, and you can rest assured I won't be letting it slide. But you have to understand, I pick my battles carefully where that kid is concerned. If she can read, write and add up, I'm satisfied. If she can't cook or speak French, I won't lose sleep."

I wanted to slap the smug look right off his perfect face. I also wanted to reach across my desk and hug him. I'd long felt sorry for Alex. He was far too young to be burdened with the responsibility of raising a sixteen-year old girl.

"Are you planning to sort this out?" I waved my page of notes at him.

He grinned. "Of course I am."

"How?" I was curious to know.

"I have my ways."

I couldn't help laughing at him, which was probably a mistake. It brought out the flirty side of him.

"You're very pretty, especially when you smile," he said quietly. "You should do it more often."

"I'll have you know I smile all the time," I defended. "Just not in the presence of you or your sister."

He laughed, a superb deep sound that matched his voice. "Give me the work Charli missed."

"Excuse me?"

He held out his hand. "Give me the assignments she missed and I'll have her do them. They'll be on your desk on Monday."

I leaned to the side and opened my desk drawer. "I'll believe it when I see it," I muttered, thumbing through the papers inside.

"Oh, ye of little faith," he crowed, snatching the papers from me as soon as I held them out. "She'll do it."

"Well, if she does, I'll be very impressed."

Alex stood up, preparing to leave. "Impressed enough to go out to dinner with me?"

My heart seemed to falter at the suggestion. Flirty innuendo from Alex was nothing new. Actually asking me out was, and I wasn't prepared for it.

A witty reply was never going to happen. "Yes."

He walked toward the door. "Great. It's a date."

"No it's not," I retorted, making him turn back. "She hasn't completed the work yet."

He waved the papers I'd given him. "Monday."

2.TENSION

There were only two places in town that sold coffee. One squirted canned cream into instant coffee and called it a cappuccino. I'm French. That automatically made such a concoction intolerable.

Alex made decent coffee, which left me with no choice when it came to choosing cafés.

"Good morning, Gabrielle," he greeted.

"Mr Blake," I replied, nodding just once.

He smiled at me. "The usual?"

"Yes, please." I pulled out a stool and sat down at the counter while he set about making my latte.

"So, I was thinking," he began, glancing back at me. "I think we need to change the terms of our date."

"Is that so?" I replied, totally unfazed. As far as I was concerned, there would be no date.

He turned around and placed a cup of coffee in front of me. "Absolutely so. Instead of going out for dinner, we should keep it on the down low. You can cook me dinner at your place," he audaciously suggested. "I don't think we should advertise the fact that we're infatuated with each other."

Infatuated? Ridiculous!

I was not infatuated with this man, and I was a hundred percent sure no part of him felt infatuated by me. From what I'd heard, Alex Blake considered women to be sport. I hate sport.

"It won't even get that far so I shan't worry."

"Shan't?" He grinned inciting a scowl from me. "You shan't worry?"

I felt crippled by the heat rising in my cheeks. English is not my first language. Much of my English education had come from reading Tolstoy novels. Anna Karenina had no aversion to the word 'shan't'.

"It's a word, Alex," I growled. "Look it up."

"Of course it's a word. I think it's a lovely word. I shan't make fun again."

He winked across at me and I wish he hadn't. It made staying furious with him difficult.

Perhaps I'd set the mood anyway. A few seconds later, the glass door of the café swung open and his sister stormed in. She obviously had no problem with being furious with him.

"How did you get here?" he asked.

"Nicole drove me," she snapped.

"Okay. Why are you here? You're supposed to be at home."

"Because you locked the shed," she spat, marching over to him. "Why would you lock me out of the shed?"

He walked around the counter perfectly calmly, which seemed to rile her even more. "Why are you so surprised? I warned you I was going to do it."

"Give me the key." She held out her hand.

"No."

"I just want my board, Alex.... any board," she whined. "I don't even care which one. Just let me in to get one."

"Have you done your homework?" he asked, lowering his tone.

The obnoxious girl was so angry she was shaking. "No."

Alex turned around and walked back behind the counter. "No surf for you then. Shame, really. The swell was outstanding this morning."

Charli glanced across at me, seemingly noticing me for the first time. "Can I have an extension, please Mademoiselle Décarie?" She spoke in the sweetest tone I'd ever heard from her.

Seeking instruction, I glanced at Alex. He infinitesimally shook his head at me.

"I saw that, Alex!" yelled Charli, abandoning the sugary tone.

"You're not getting an extension, Charlotte," he said quietly. "You've already been given an extension."

Charli straightened up and drew in a long breath. Even I could tell she was plotting her next move. "Fine," she relented. "I'm going to spend the day at the cliffs then. I'll kill the whole weekend taking pictures."

"If you say so, Charli."

"I'm going to hitchhike up there, Alex," she threatened.

"No you won't," he told her. "Besides, it would be a wasted trip."

She narrowed her hazel eyes. "Why?"

"Because I locked your camera in the shed too," he said smugly. "I've clipped your bratty wings. Now go home and get your French work done."

I'd never been victorious where Charli was concerned but Alex was clearly used to it. He barely batted an eyelid as she stormed out of the café muttering under her breath.

"Is it always like that?" I asked curiously.

If that kind of tension were commonplace, he probably wouldn't survive her teenage years.

"You might not believe me, but it's hardly ever like that," he replied. "We get along well most of the time."

"If you say so," I mumbled, bringing my cup to my lips.

He grinned broadly. "Today's going to get worse before it gets better."

"Why?"

"She owes Mrs Jennings an essay too. I just haven't told her yet."

3. A DEAL IS A DEAL

The last thing I expected was for Charli to actually come through. The sullen girl stalked into class on Monday morning and slammed three completed essays down on my desk.

I spent my lunch hour grading them. It wasn't brilliant but she'd earned a passing grade. As usual, Charli Blake had done the bare minimum to scrape through. If she were mine, I'd smack her.

A deal is a deal, and because of that, I spent the entire afternoon making a grand dinner. Determined to dazzle Alex with my French culinary skills, I made coq au vin. I set a perfect table, going to the extra effort of picking a bunch of peonies for the centrepiece.

I loved my garden. I'd never been particularly green thumbed but whoever owned it before me was. It was the epitome of a traditional cottage garden – almost English in design. Regardless of the season, there was always something flowering.

My efforts would undoubtedly be wasted on Alex Blake. The vase of peonies would probably last longer than the so-called infatuation he held for me. Despite this, I spent ten minutes ironing the white tablecloth and napkins.

He arrived at exactly eight o'clock.

"You're on time," I praised. "I'm impressed."

Smiling brightly, he produced a bottle of wine and a small bunch of flowers from behind his back. I recognised them immediately. He'd stolen them from my garden on the way up to the porch.

"Thank you, I've never seen such lovely flowers," I mocked, taking the loose bunch from him.

"Really?" he asked, grinning cheekily. "I swiped them from outside. There's plenty more."

Smiling because I had no choice, I ushered him through the door.

Alex walked to the centre of the lounge room, making no secret of the fact that he was checking out my home. An easel standing near the front window caught his attention. He ambled over to it and leaned down, studying the half finished painting. "Talented and beautiful," he declared, glancing back at me. "That's a stellar combination."

"Your sweet-talk is wasted on me, Alex," I declared. "I know how you operate."

He slowly ambled toward me, looking more curious than outraged. "You do? You're on to me already?"

I couldn't be sure he was joking. "Yes. Sabine Daintree told me all about you."

He cringed at the mention of her name, and rightly so.

I'd met Sabine at Pilates class. The residents of Pipers Cove weren't exactly into physical contrology. It was a tiny class, which gave us plenty of time to talk. I knew all about her whirlwind three-week romance with Alex Blake. At the time, she'd been besotted with him. The enchantment quickly wore off when he heartlessly dumped her on Christmas Eve.

There was no way my fate would be the same.

"I'll bet she told you everything," he said drawing out the words.

"Yes, so you needn't try so hard to win me over." I tried to sound strong but he was making it difficult. He stood close enough that I could smell him. A lovely spicy scent that I couldn't quite pinpoint was driving me crazy. "You and I will go no further than this night."

"I shan't waste my time then," he teased, taking a step closer to me. "And to think, I was going to propose after dinner."

I took a step back because the position I was in was a dangerous one. I'd left Manhattan to escape a wildly attractive smooth talker. I wasn't about to fall prey to another one.

"Well, you'll be pleased to know that I would've declined your offer."

A slow smile swept his face. "Sabine Daintree has four dogs," he said irrelevantly.

"So?"

"So, I'm allergic to dogs," he replied. "I tried and I tried but I needed a dose of antihistamines to be within a ten foot radius of her, but I'm guessing she left that part out when explaining what a bastard I was."

I straightened my pose, feeling slightly foolish. "She said you'd been unwilling to compromise."

Perhaps I should have asked her for more details.

"I couldn't compromise." He grinned. "Every time I went near her I blew up like a balloon. It wasn't a good look for me."

I giggled at his daft comment.

"Do you have a dog?" he asked, glancing around the room.

"I might consider getting one if you continue with your run of silliness."

"Silliness?" he teased.

I felt the familiar burn of embarrassment again. "If you're going to keep teasing me – "

"I don't mean to tease you, Gabrielle, really," he assured, stepping closer to me again. "I think your words are lovely. I think you're lovely, but you know that."

I wondered where this was headed. We were adults — two sensible, consenting adults. I was over cocky, egotistical men but it didn't mean I couldn't have a bit of fun with one.

"Where do you see this going, Alex?"

"Do you need a five year plan?" he asked, looking slightly worried. "I'm not big on five year plans. In fact, two month plans stress me out."

I shook my head. "What about a one night plan? Do you have any problems making a one night plan?"

"Are you offering me a one night plan, Gabrielle?" His low voice sent a rush of desire through me.

"Not yet," I replied, surprising myself. "For now, I'm offering you dinner."

***

Coq au vin wasn't a dish that Alex was familiar with. He told me it was the best chicken stew he'd ever had. I could overlook his backward compliment because the rest of the conversation was wonderful.

He wasn't the one-dimensional beach bum I'd expected him to be. He was witty, funny and charming. And I was in big trouble because of it.

I stood up and began to clear the table, mainly to stop myself looking at him. Alex followed me into the kitchen.

Obviously he wasn't as enamoured as I was. His focus was on my kitchen cupboards. "Why is that door crooked?" he asked, stooping down to open it.

I placed the dishes on the edge of the sink. "It's always been broken," I replied.

Just as he stood up, I turned around. Bumping into him wasn't intentional – but not moving out of the way was. Alex Blake was officially driving me crazy. I could feel my whole body seizing up.

"Do you have a screwdriver?" he mumbled, focusing on my mouth.

"Somewhere," I stuttered.

A slow smile crept across his face. "Do you want to get it for me?" he asked quietly. "I'll fix it."

"I think you should leave it until the morning."

I'd left him with two choices. He could either make a run for the door or read between the lines. I held my breath while he deliberated.

"What if I want an extension on the one night plan?" he asked, leaning in so close that I felt his words.

"I'm not renowned for giving extensions," I whispered.

"At least give me the opportunity to change your mind."

I didn't ask how. I let him to show me. When he pushed the shoulder strap of my dress aside and pressed his warm lips against my décolletage, my legs began to fail me. I was now in really big trouble – and didn't care one bit. I craned my neck as he kissed a long slow line toward my mouth.

"Ah, this probably isn't appropriate behaviour considering we're in a kitchen," I mumbled.

"Has anyone ever told you that you talk too much?" He hummed the words against my throat, sending a lovely shudder through me.

"A few people," I breathed. "I don't usually take any notice."

He let out a low laugh. "Shut up, Gabrielle."

"Make me shut up, Alex."

Accepting the challenge, he silenced me with a long kiss, wandering hands and his magnificent body.

4. FUNNY WAYS

Waking up alone wasn't a good sign. In fact, it was devastating. One-night stands weren't usually my style, which probably explained why I felt so wretched. I hadn't even heard him leave. I tried hard not to picture Alex creeping out of my bed at dawn, grateful for the escape. I had no right to be upset. The terms of our agreement had been very clear. It was a one-night deal.

I went to the café later that morning, just as I had almost every morning for the past year. I wasn't expecting a full play-by-play of the night before, but I wasn't expecting to be given the cold shoulder either.

Alex did a double-take as I walked in, and then asked Nicole to make my coffee. "I just need to check something out the back," he muttered unconvincingly.

He was gone before I had a chance to speak. I ignored the overwhelming urge to hysterically cry and run out the door. I tried hard to make polite conversation with Nicole instead. I didn't know the girl well. French wasn't one of her classes.

"Where's Charli today?" It was the best I could come up with. One was rarely seen without the other.

"With Mitchell Tate." She rolled her eyes. "He's leaving town soon and she's making the most of having him around."

"Are they romantically involved?" I asked.

I was used to the sly grins I received when speaking to teenagers. Alex wasn't the first to point out that my choice of words were less than conventional.

"No," she scoffed. "She just likes surfing with him because he can get her out past the break. She can't go alone."

"I see."

I didn't really. I had no clue what she meant.

"How will she get out there after he leaves?" I asked naively.

Nicole carelessly slid a cup of coffee across the counter. I put my hand on the edge of the counter, managing to save it from hitting the floor.

"She won't," she said bleakly. "But she'll probably give it a crack anyway."

***

I spent the rest of the day painting. It's all I could think of doing to take my mind off the huge miss-step I'd taken the night before. Pushing it to the back of my mind became impossible when Alex Blake's loutish red Ute pulled onto my driveway.

I kept jabbing away at the canvas in front of me, paying him no attention as he stepped up onto the veranda.

"Hello, Gabs," he greeted.

In my twenty-five years on earth, no one had ever referred to me as Gabs. It was the most ridiculous thing I'd ever heard.

I grunted out my reply. "Hello. What do you want?"

I could see him from the corner of my eye, leaning against a veranda post with his arms folded, smiling like he'd won something. For a quick moment, I considered turning around and painting a big L on his forehead.

"Are you mad at me?"

I spun around to face him and hit him with a slew of French insults that would've made my mother blush. It didn't exactly have the desired effect. He stalked toward me smiling brightly. His arm snaked around my waist and I quickly struggled free.

"First you sneak out of my bed at dawn and then you ignore me. Of course I'm mad."

"Firstly, I didn't sneak out at dawn," he explained. "I snuck out before midnight. You were sleeping. I guess I wore you out."

I turned around and dropped my brush into a jar of turpentine. The urge to brand him was growing stronger by the second.

"Before midnight?" I sounded appalled. "You really are a pig!"

"But I'm a responsible pig, Gabs," he defended. "I'm not in the habit of leaving a sixteen-year-old kid to her own devices all night. I had to go home."

It was a perfectly legitimate excuse but it did nothing to dissolve the chagrin I was feeling.

"You could've told me that last night," I grumbled, looking to the floor.

Alex reached out, lightly pinching my chin between his thumb and forefinger. He tilted my head giving me no option but to look at him. "I'm sorry. I should've told you."

"And why did you ignore me when I came to the café?"

Releasing his hold on me, he pulled a face as if I'd reminded him of something horrible. "I'm not quite sure how this is going to play out, Gabrielle," he said quietly. "I don't want to curse things. I think we have a better chance of making things work if we just keep it to ourselves for a while. This is new territory for me."

A strange groan escaped me. "I don't like secrets," I spat. "I'm certainly not going to be one."

Alex turned around and paced a few steps away from me, blowing out a long breath while he pieced his next sentence together. "I'm just asking for a little time. I like you Gabrielle, you have to believe that."

"You have a funny way of showing it," I muttered.

He turned back to face me. "I have lots of funny ways. I have no choice. My situation is very complicated."

I knew the situation he was speaking of. She was the demanding little diva whose bad attitude marred my every day. I found it incredibly unfair that he'd been lumbered with such baggage.

"I'm sure Charli wants you to be happy," I reasoned.

"She does, and I am," he insisted. "But I'm not going to jump headfirst into anything until I can be sure you can deal with it. I'm not free and easy. I have responsibilities."

"And if I can't deal with it?"

"Then I will walk away and you'll be thankful that no one ever knew we spent time together," he said glumly.

"That's it? You wouldn't even try to make it work?"

He shook his head. "I can't promise you everything, Gabrielle. I'm not capable of giving you everything right now."

"Because of Charli?"

He cringed as I said it. Perhaps I'd put a sour spin on her name.

"You're not going to want to hear it, but she comes first. It's been that way for a long time."

Part of me wanted to run inside and lock the door. Any man who put his life on hold for the sake of his bratty younger sister was a little off kilter. A bigger part of me wanted a repeat performance of the night before. There was something special about Alex Blake, and I wanted to hang in there long enough to find out what it was.

5. SICK DAY

For someone who'd claimed not to like secrets, I was enjoying ours far too much. I saw Alex every day, usually more than once. He was a creature of habit. I'd wake up every morning and make a beeline for the lounge room windows. Without fail, I'd see him hundreds of yards off shore chasing waves.

Despite the fact that it screamed stalker, I'd gone as far as buying binoculars so I could get a better look. I liked studying Alex. The man with a wildly complicated home life found complete solace in the ocean.

The evil sister did too. I liked to study Charli as well – when she was half a mile off shore and I couldn't hear her.

Their routine was always the same. She'd trail behind her brother, paddling hard to get to where they needed to be. Eventually Alex would stop and let her catch up. He led her through the ocean the same way he led her through life, always stopping to let her catch up.

Alex's take hadn't been so poetic when I mentioned it to him. "She's only small, Gabs," he replied. "It's a long way to paddle."

As much as she grated on me, Charli really didn't impede on the time I spent with Alex, probably because she knew nothing about it. We'd steal a moment in the mornings when I went to the café for coffee and thanks to Charli's out of control social schedule, most weekends were our own.

Wednesdays were not usually our day so I was surprised when Alex turned up at my door just after eight o'clock.

"What are you doing here?" I asked, grabbing his hand and pulling him through the door.

Alex pulled me in and kissed me as if it had been weeks since we'd seen each other. "I have the whole day planned," he murmured. "Let's go."

Breaking free of his hold on me, I giggled. "I have to be at school in twenty minutes."

"Are you sure?" he asked, drawing out the words. "You don't look very well." He put his hand to my forehead. "You might be coming down with something."

I brushed his hand away. "Really?" I asked, playing along.

"Yes. You should call in sick, just to be sure."

I'd never faked a sick day in my life. I wasn't even sure how. Alex obviously had a few ideas. He coached me through the phone call before I'd dialled the number.

Tiffany, the school's admin assistant answered. I coughed a little bit, explained how ill I was and told her that my lessons were in a daily planner on my desk. She didn't even question it. Instead she wished me well and told me to get better soon.

I felt horribly guilty, right up until Alex pulled me into his arms and promised me a wonderful day.

"Where are we going?" I asked, trying to remain upright as he pressed his lips to the side of my neck.

He straightened up and smiled at me, doing nothing to help me hold my ground. "We're going to the beach."

I felt a little deflated. I loved to look at the beach – or paint the beach. Trudging along it and getting sand in my shoes held no appeal.

I linked my arms around his neck and gave my best pouty look. "We could just stay here for the day," I suggested.

He swooped down and kissed me hard on the lips. "Nice try, sweetheart. Let's go."

A day at the beach was bad enough but what Alex had in mind was much worse. I knew it wasn't going to be good when he started unloading gear from the tray of the Ute.

When he handed me a black wetsuit, I began to panic. "What do I need this for?"

He glanced back at me, grinning. "We're going surfing," he replied casually. "You keep telling me that you can't see what all the fuss is about. I'm going to show you."

"No, no, no." I grabbed his arm in a plea for understanding. "I don't surf."

Perplexed by my panic, he stopped what he was doing, turned around and took my face in his hands. "I'll teach you. The water's perfectly calm and this will keep you warm." He patted the wetsuit he'd given me.

Alex was nothing if not persistent. Despite my protests, we ended up at the water's edge just a few minutes later. I looked to the sky, praying for a massive storm and then thought better of it. It would probably spur the adrenaline junkie on even more. When he started pulling on his wetsuit, I knew I'd reached the end of the line.

"Let's go, Gabs." He reached behind his back, dragging the zipper upward. "Chop, chop."

I shook my head. "No. I refuse."

Grinning slyly, he stalked through the sand toward me. "You refuse? I'm offering to let you in on the secret of universe and you refuse? I'm gutted."

"What secret?" I scoffed.

"Peace," he swooped his arm around me and pulled me in close, "love, harmony, all that good stuff."

I was feeling perfectly peaceful until he'd dragged me to the beach.

"No. Let me go," I demanded. "This very minute."

Alex didn't let me go. In a move I could never have predicted, he scooped me up and began carrying me toward the water. By the time we got there, I was rigid with fear.

"Stop," I whimpered, "right now."

Finally picking up on my terror, Alex stopped dead in his tracks. He lowered me to my feet and I crumpled in a heap on the sand, sobbing like a little girl.

He sat down beside me, pulling my head against his chest.

"What's wrong?" He sounded as panicked as I felt. "Tell me."

I swallowed hard, trying to get the words out. My first attempt sounded like gibberish so I tried again. "I can't swim."

Big masses of water that looked like they could swallow me whole incited immediate fear. It was irrational and embarrassing and something I'd never been able to conquer.

He pulled away from me and lifted my chin, chasing my eyes. "Why didn't you tell me?" he asked softly.

"It never came up," I muttered, still struggling to pull myself together.

There was nothing I could do to stop the tears rolling down my cheeks. I felt pathetic.

"I am such a dick," he muttered, brushing my cheeks with his thumbs. "I'm so sorry, Gabs. I had no idea."

"It's okay," I replied. "I never told you."

My secret was out. I wasn't the fearless warrior princess a man like Alex probably wanted. I was a wimpy spoiled princess with a penchant for books about art and expensive shoes. If he'd dumped me back at my cottage and run for the hills, I wouldn't have blamed him. But Alex didn't run.

He took me back to the cottage and straight to bed, which is where we stayed for the rest of the day.

6.SOCIAL SUICIDE

I loved my job with the exception of one particular class. The rowdy group of year elevens I faced that morning were a motley bunch. A handful of students actually wanted to be there but the majority saw my class as somewhere to pass time – a bludge session, as they called it.

I walked in and quickly scanned the room. I could gauge how difficult the hour was going to be based on who'd bothered to show up. Almost half of the class seemed to be missing. It didn't even upset me anymore.

"Right," I announced, slamming a book down on my desk. "Eyes to the front."

Everyone twisted in their seats, giving me the impression I had control of the room. It was fleeting.

Charli Blake strolled in the door a minute later. I didn't particularly care that she was late. What riled me was the fact that she said nothing by way of excuse or apology. She just ambled down the aisle between the rows of desks as if she was the queen of the whole world.

"Stop walking," I ordered.

A pin drop could've been heard as she slowly turned back to face me.

"Why are you late?"

She shrugged. "No reason."

"Well, considering that you have no respect for my time, I'll assume that you'll have no problem sharing some of yours with me this afternoon," I told her. "See you in detention."

Her already big brown eyes grew wider. "Today?"

"Yes, today."

After thinking it through for a long moment, the obnoxious girl waved her hands, bowed down and curtsied. "As you wish, Mademoiselle."

As expected, her juvenile display earned her a round of stifled giggles from her teammates.

I loudly shushed them, demanding silence.

Charli continued on her way, pulled out a chair at the desk farthest from mine and sat down. I braved her baleful glare for the rest of the hour. Never before had a student rattled me the way she did.

I never told Alex about her antics. It would only serve as more worry for him. He'd confided that the evil sister was wreaking more havoc than usual of late and he had no clue why. I certainly had no answers for him. As far as I was concerned, she'd always been an insolent witch.

***

When Charli failed to show up for detention, I knew I had no choice but to clue Alex in. I'd planned to tell him when he came for dinner the next night but the second I opened the door to him, I knew there probably wasn't going to be a good time to broach the subject.

"What's the matter?" I asked, grabbing his hand and pulling him inside. Alex looked completely broken. I expected to hear something truly dreadful. He didn't even kiss me. He trudged across to the centre of the room, leaving me hanging.

I closed the front door and leaned my back against it as if I was barricading us inside. "Say something, please," I begged.

After a long minute of silence, he flopped down on the nearest sofa, rested both elbows on his knees and buried his face in his hands.

I moved to sit beside him.

"Some days I have no clue what I'm doing," he muttered.

I gripped his wrist, unsuccessfully trying to pull his hands free of his face. "I don't know what you mean."

"How am I supposed to deal with her? Do you know, Gabi?" he asked desperately. "If you can give me any insight into what the hell spins through the mind of a sixteen-year-old girl, I'd love to hear it."

I let go of him and slumped back in the cushion. "What has she done?"

I shouldn't have sounded as irate as I did, especially considering the story he went on to tell me was so tragic.

"She was supposed to stay at Nicole Lawson's last night," he choked. "Imagine how it felt finding out that she spent the night at Mitchell Tate's dive of a shack."

"She told you this?" I asked warily. I couldn't imagine Charli volunteering that kind of information, especially to Alex.

He finally lifted his head to look at me. "No. Jasmine told me. She couldn't wait to bring me up to speed," he said bitterly.

My mind reeled as I tried to come up with something supportive to say. "Alex, I know that – "

He jumped off the chair and cut me off with a disgruntled growl. "She's sixteen, Gabrielle! I could understand it if she was in a relationship with him but there was nothing!" he ranted. "It's all around town. Why would she do something like that?"

He looked absolutely stricken. I had no answers for him. I forged ahead anyway, trying to calm him. "It will pass. Gossip is always fleeting."

He spun back to face me. "Do you really believe that?"

No, I didn't believe it. I had a sinking feeling that Charli Blake had just committed social suicide.

7.DRAMA

I didn't see Alex again that weekend. He spent two days holed up with Charli at home. They didn't even go to the beach. My heart broke, and not just for him. I'd been in Pipers Cove long enough to know it was going to take Charli years to live down the mistake she'd made.

None of us were immune to errors in judgement and a dose of humiliation can be a great driving force when it comes to moving forward. The problem was, I didn't think sixteen-year-old girls had the wisdom to see it.

No one expected her to show up to school on Monday, least of all me. I expected fifth period French to be the toughest for her. It was the last class of the day and from what I'd heard at lunchtime, the torment had been constant since nine o'clock. Year eleven French was the worst of the worst as far as wretches go.

If she'd failed to show up, not even I would've blamed her – but she did show. I wanted to leap of out my seat and offer her an armed escort as she walked in the door. She looked terrible – the kind of look that comes after crying solidly for two days.

The whole room fell silent as Charli slowly took the walk of shame down the aisle to her desk at the back of the class. I thought she'd pulled it off until a boy cowardly called her a slut and tried masking it with a fake cough.

"Who said that?" I demanded.

No one owned up. I felt the best plan of attack from there would be to quickly move on. I ordered them to take out their books and copy the notes on the board.

Charli sat down trying her best to appear unaffected by the cruel words. I knew better. She was blinking at a rate of knots, desperately trying to stop the tears spilling over. She didn't speak for the whole lesson and made the wise move of making sure she was the last to leave at the end of class.

I called out to her as she passed my desk. "You owe me a detention, Charli," I said quietly.

She stared blankly at me. It was then that I noticed there wasn't a hint of colour in her ashen cheeks. Charli Blake was a brat, but she'd always been a pretty brat. Today she looked barely recognisable.

She didn't even attempt to sass me. Instead, she walked to the nearest desk and dumped her bag down. "You can have me," she muttered, slumping down on the chair. "I have nowhere to be."

***

I managed to find reason to detain her afterschool every other day for three weeks. Alex knew all about my strategy. He also knew it was doing very little to save her from the mindless torment. Charli slowly withdrew from the world and he was terrified for her. We spent hours on end talking about it.

"This is the point where you're supposed to tell me it's too hard, Gabs," he said, only half jokingly.

I put my hand to his cheek, turning his face toward me. "I'm not going anywhere," I insisted. "I happen to think you're worth it. This is temporary."

I was telling the truth, but it didn't mean I always understood his need to take Charli's drama onboard. I'd observed it from a distance for months.

It wasn't a traditional brother and sister relationship. Most of the time, Alex had an authoritative hold over Charli. He struggled hard to keep her in line and for the most part, she accepted it. I suspected that was why seeing her fall so far off track was so devastating to him.

"Do you think we're temporary?" he asked cautiously.

I moved my hand, trailing my fingers along his stubbly cheek. "No, I think we're fine. I miss you though, terribly."

I felt his whole body tense through my hand. "I know we haven't spent a lot of time together lately," he said quietly. "I just need to keep a close eye on her until – "

I put my finger to his lips. "I'm not going anywhere."

"Why do you put up with me?" he murmured beneath my finger. "This isn't your problem."

I dropped my hand to my lap and shrugged. "I cannot explain why, except to say that love makes us do all sorts of unreasonable things."

He smiled for the first time in weeks. "You love me?"

It wasn't a declaration I'd planned to make so soon but it was too late to take the words back. "I can't find reason not to."

He put his hand behind my neck and pulled me forward. His mouth easily found mine and before I knew what was happening, we'd found a temporary escape from the drama.

***

Almost a month after the scandal of the century broke, Charli started to show signs of recovery. In a tiny but important step, she'd agreed to spend the night at her best friend Nicole's house.

Alex was reluctant to let her go but I argued that it would be a good break for both of them. My motives weren't entirely pure. Without Charli to watch over, he was mine for the entire night.

I made the absolute most of it, starting with a stellar chicken chasseur.

"I love your chicken stews," praised Alex.

I smiled across the table at him. "Just so you know, I have never served you stew."

"I know." He grinned back at me and I realised he'd been teasing me all along. "They're more like casseroles."

I shook my head. "You're incorrigible."

His smile slowly started to fade and the conversation took a serious turn. "Don't give up on me, Gabs."

"Why would I ever do that?"

Alex reached across the table for my hand. I met him half way. "Will you skive work tomorrow?"

I frowned. "I do not know what skive means."

"Call in sick," he explained, grinning again. "Spend the whole day with me."

"That depends," I replied. "If I spend the whole day with you tomorrow, will you spend the whole night with me tonight?"

"You have to ask?"

"I've never woken up with you in my bed, Alex."

He frowned at me as if it was something he'd only just realised. He held my hand tighter. "I am so sorry," he murmured. "Don't give up on me."

***

I woke three times during the night, subconsciously expecting Alex's side of the bed to be empty. But he was there each time, looking as handsome as I'd ever seen him.

The worried frown was noticeably absent, which made me happy. I was beginning to think it was going to become permanently etched across his forehead. He looked young and momentarily free of the drama that plagued him while he was awake.

Feeling a sudden urge to be closer to him, I snuggled in and rested my head on his chest.

"I love you, Gabs," he whispered, raking his fingers through my hair.

"Say it again," I whispered back.

"I love you, Gabs."

I turned my head, kissed his warm chest, closed my eyes and went back to sleep.

8. BLACK RIVER

I was becoming quite skilled at calling in sick to my job. I'd done it twice in three months. That made doing it a third time a breeze. I stuck with my usual lie, feigning a terrible coughing fit before claiming to have the flu.

"You should really get that cough checked out, Gabrielle," urged Tiffany.

"I will," I croaked. "I'll see you tomorrow."

Alex received a text message from Charli, assuring him that she'd gone to school. She was a smart girl. She'd thought to attach a photo as proof.

That freed us up to have a wonderful day together with no worries, but when we arrived at his destination of choice I wasn't confident that it would happen.

We'd driven an hour south and ended up at a river. I was devastated and wasted no time in telling him so. "Take me home." I didn't sound as angry as I'd hoped.

Alex turned off the ignition and reached for my hand. "Do you trust me, Gabrielle?"

"Unless you're planning to throw me in the river you have no reason to ask me such a thing," I replied, finally sounding irate.

He unclipped his seatbelt and leaned toward me. "I'm going to teach you to swim, if you'll let me."

I felt my heart start galloping at the mere thought. I stared through the windscreen at the water. It wasn't even pretty water. It was ominously jet black and inky.

"In that?" I asked, horrified. "Look at the water!"

Alex's hand moved to the back of my head, rubbing my scalp with his fingertips in a ploy to calm me down. "I promise you, if you don't like it, we'll leave."

I already knew I wasn't going to like it but it wasn't going to get that far. My irrational fear of drowning would prevent me from setting foot anywhere near the water.

"No. I'm not doing it." The words came out sounding much rougher than I'd planned.

Alex straightened up in the seat and spent an abnormally long time staring ahead at the water. "Okay," he said finally. "You'll just have to wait here then."

"Why? Where are you going?"

He opened the door and began to get out of the car. "Swimming."

***

Even I had to admit that he'd chosen the perfect day for it. The weather was fine and the day was bright. It wasn't exactly warm but Tasmania rarely is. Locals like the Blakes' seemed to have a high tolerance to low water temperatures. If the sun was shining, it was a good enough excuse to hit the water. Most of the time they were sensible enough to don a thick enough layer of neoprene to protect themselves against the chill.

Alex seemed to have lost his mind that day.

I watched through the windscreen in absolute disbelief as he stripped off every piece of clothing. He stood on the bank of the river wearing nothing more than a bulletproof look on his face. I couldn't even look away. He was truly a perfect specimen of a man.

"What are you doing?" I shrieked through the open window.

His grin broadened and he threw out his arms. "I'm going swimming. Come with me."

I furiously shook my head. "Never!"

I giggled then because I couldn't help myself.

"Last chance," he warned, taking a few backward steps toward the water.

I couldn't take my eyes off him. I couldn't take my mind off him either. I might not have been brave enough to venture into the water, but I was brave enough to try and coax him out.

I got out of the Ute and slammed the door hard, making sure I had his full attention.

"You've changed your mind?" he asked sceptically.

One at a time, I kicked off my shoes and continued walking toward him. "No. I am firm in my decision."

His wide smile would have been visible from space. "So what are you doing then?"

I peeled off my shirt and tossed it to the ground, secretly hoping it wouldn't get dirt on it. "What does it look like I'm doing?" I asked haughtily. "I'm disrobing."

I could tell that he'd tried his hardest not to laugh – for at least a second. "Disrobing?" he repeated. "I love it when you talk dirty, Gabs."

I was paying too much attention to Alex and not enough to where I was walking. The sharp stone I stepped on made the decision to take my shoes off a bad one. I stumbled to the side, somehow managing not to fall over.

"Do you want me to come and get you?" called Alex.

"No," I quickly replied. "I cannot trust you not to throw me in the dirty river."

Alex didn't try hiding his laugh this time. It was so loud that I heard it echo across the water. "It's not dirty," he said finally composing himself.

I was close enough to get a good look at it by that stage. It looked positively toxic and no less black than it had looked from the car.

I shimmied out of my skirt, keeping my eyes on the water the whole time.

"It looks like a giant bowl of cola," I complained. "It's filthy."

"The tannin makes the water brown," he explained. "It's organic. Look at the trees on the banks. See how they grow right into the water?"

I looked to the edge of the water on the far side of the river. There was no bank. The thick bush ended where the water began.

"The tannin seeps out of the bark. That's what colours the water," he continued.

"Are you sure that is true?"

"That's the scientific explanation." He grinned at me. "But I know a better one."

"You do?"

"Yes."

"Tell me," I demanded.

"Finish disrobing first," he teased. "You're only half way there."

I looked down, suddenly acutely aware that I was dressed in nothing more than my underwear. The only positive I could find is that my bra and panties almost matched.

I looked toward Alex who was now just a few yards away, still standing buck naked at the waters edge. "My plan was to get naked and coax you out of going swimming," I revealed.

"Well, it's never going to work now, is it?" he asked slyly. "You've just lost the upper hand by telling me your game plan."

I gave it my best shot anyway. I unhooked my bra and dropped it to the ground. "All you have to do is come over here and you can have me," I taunted.

His smile didn't waver. "I already have you."

Damn, he was good.

All I had left between victory and me was my panties, but I didn't feel like I was winning. After a quick glance around to make sure no one was around, I slipped them off and tossed them at Alex. They missed him by a mile and landed in the dirt but he didn't seem to notice.

"You are so bloody beautiful," he told me.

"Thank you," I replied, walking toward him. "Now tell me your version of why the water looks like black tea," I demanded, taking his hand as he reached out to me.

"I'll tell you when we're in the water."

"No, Alex." I shrugged free and turned around with the intention of hightailing it back to the car. His firm arm looped around my middle, stopping me from taking a single step. I could feel the warmth radiating off his body as he held my back to his chest. "Why are you so afraid?" he whispered in my ear.

"Because I can't swim," I replied shakily. "I'll drown."

"I promise to keep a firm hold on you," he told me. "There is no way you're going to drown today. Walk with me."

Our feet shuffled in the dirt as he turned us around to face the water. "Baby steps, Alex," I muttered.

We took short steps forward until we were standing knee deep in the water. It was so cold that it made me suck in a sharp breath.

"Still want to hear my story?" he asked, humming the words against the side of my neck.

"Yes." My voice sounded tiny and terrified.

"It's about a couple of fairies called Tansi and Rhosyn," he began.

Fairies? Perhaps the cold water was making him delirious.

"Nonsense," I whimpered.

"Hear me out," he urged. "Tansi had a pretty spectacular job. She was in charge of making sand jewels."

I'd never heard of sand jewels. Even after all this time there were still many English terms that confounded me.

In a shaky voice, I asked him to explain it to me. "What do they look like?"

"I don't know, I've never seen one," he replied. "Legend has it that they're the most beautiful, bright jewels on earth, but they're extraordinarily rare. Very few people have seen one."

"You're making this up," I scoffed, still trembling.

"I'm not," he insisted. "Tansi would spend months gathering sand and making it into jewels. Then she'd have to hide them."

"Why?"

"Because sand jewels are the most precious gem on earth, and each one takes 709 years to make."

I could overlook the very precise manufacturing time he'd given me. For some reason, I was more curious as to how they were made. He didn't skip a beat when I asked him. It almost made me believe he wasn't making it up as he went along.

"Tansi sources the finest sand and moulds it into the shape of the jewel. Then it has to cure."

"For 709 years," I said dryly.

I felt his smile against my bare shoulder. "Exactly. But she had a problem. Rhosyn was an evil thief. Every time Tansi hid the jewels in the bush to cure, Rhosyn would find them."

"She should have hidden them better," I muttered.

"It wouldn't have made any difference," he replied. "When sand jewels are fully cured, they're impossibly bright – and adding to her troubles was the fact that Rhosyn could fly. She used to fly high above, scanning the bush below. Once each jewel cured and started twinkling, Rhosyn would swipe it."

"That's horrible. Poor Tansi."

"I know, right?" He laughed. "It was 709 years of hard work down the drain."

"So what did she do?"

"Well, Rhosyn might have had the wings but Tansi had the magic. She came up with the idea of hiding them in the rivers," he explained. "But there was a problem."

"They shone through the water?"

"Yes they did, right up until she wove some magic and turned the water black. It hid them perfectly. Rhosyn used to fly overhead searching for the sand jewels, never having a clue that they were hidden under the blackened water the whole time."

I twisted in his arms, suddenly desperate to see his eyes. "Whatever became of her? Rhosyn, I mean."

"She still searches to this day. I'm sure you've seen her."

"What does she look like?"

"Well, what do you think she'd look like?"

I thought hard, trying to picture a kleptomaniac fairy with wings.

"She'd probably have short hair. No girl likes the windswept look."

Alex let out a low chuckle that sent nothing but pure desire coursing through my veins. "Can I tell you something else?" he whispered.

I nodded, keeping my focus on his hazel eyes.

He leaned down close to me, murmuring his words against my lips. "You're swimming, Gabs."

I gripped him tighter, digging my fingers into his skin while I jerked my head in every direction, quickly glancing around.

I'd been so caught up in his tale that I hadn't noticed he'd been inching us further into the water the whole time. We were at least five metres from the safety of the bank. I tried to pull away from him and stand, then gripped him tighter when I realised I couldn't.

My first inclination was to start screaming for help but I was somehow able to reason with myself. I didn't need help. Alex had a good hold on me – the best ever – we were naked. And I hadn't drowned, which probably meant I was going to live through it.

"Don't let me go," I warned.

Suddenly, the hold he had on me wasn't so polite anymore. "I'm never going to let you go," he whispered.

9. PERFECT MAN

I've kept a diary since I was fourteen years old. I now had a cupboard full of notebooks detailing every drama and hope I'd had since. Re-reading them was something I didn't do often but for some reason, I'd spent the best part of the evening parked up on the couch with a glass of wine doing just that.

One particular entry made me giggle. When I was twenty, I made a list detailing the attributes of my perfect man.

1. Must be handsome.

2. College educated or higher.

3. Fantastic sense of style and dress sense.

4. Likes books.

At the time, it was perfect. Not long after writing the list, I thought I'd found him. I was living in Manhattan, working toward an art degree and trying to better my English skills by working part-time in a library.

I met James at a party. He was a twenty-seven year old stockbroker with a penchant for designer suits and life in the fast line.

It took nearly four years for me to realise that life in the fast lane was not for me. I slowed down and he kept going. Perhaps that explained why I was totally oblivious to the fact that he was bedding half the women in Manhattan.

I was utterly convinced that I loved him, and believing he loved me too, I forgave him. I'd taken him at his word when he'd tearfully promised it would never happen again. It didn't take me long to realise I'd made a mistake. James mistook my kindness for weakness and continued breaking my heart on a daily basis.

I'm not a foolish girl. I'm not usually a vengeful girl either but there was something very therapeutic about emptying tubes of oil paint into every one of his shoes. I decided to get the hell out of Manhattan after that. I had my degree, plenty of money and no reason to stay.

A quick online search for an international teaching position took all of ten minutes. When I saw the advertisement seeking an art teacher in Tasmania, I jumped at the chance.

My mind conjured up all sorts of lovely images. I expected to spend the rest of my career teaching well-behaved children to paint in an open field under an oak tree – Little House On The Prairie style.

The reality didn't quite match up. A month after I got here, the French teacher quit and cuts were made to the art program. I was shoved into the role of Mademoiselle Décarie, French teacher.

I didn't even consider leaving. I'd found my pretty cottage by that stage and had fallen in love with the town. Pipers Cove was a fresh start and ten thousand miles from James and his oily shoes.

***

Alex Blake was nothing like the man on my list. The only pre-requisite he met was number one, and it certainly wasn't because he had fantastic dress sense and style. I didn't even consider jeans and button down shirts to be a style, but he was good and honest and nothing like the cad Sabine Daintree had accused him of being.

I no longer lived life in the fast lane. Life at Alex's pace was slow and blissful, even with the complication of Charli.

Charli eventually managed to weather the storm that her one night of stupidity had brought on, but she hadn't managed to escape unscathed. From what I could tell, she'd declared war on the Beautifuls. Despite the fact that it would probably be a long war, I got the impression she'd eventually be victorious, especially if it came down to a battle of wits.

Jasmine Tate was pure evil. She never missed an opportunity to remind Charli of her social faux pas, but her wrath wasn't one-track. She seemed to reduce at least one girl to tears every day, and I found it very telling that they were always younger than her.

Her sister was a different kettle of fish. Lily didn't seem to have two brain cells to rub together. She'd once asked me if *à la carte* referred to food that was served off a cart.

It wasn't hard to see why Charli got the better of her but that didn't mean I condoned it. When I followed Lily down the corridor on my way to the first class after lunch, I knew Charli had struck. There was a steady stream of water coming from the bottom of the bag on Lily's back – at least I hoped it was water.

For a quick moment, I considered saying nothing and letting her go on her way, but unlike Charli Blake, I had a conscience.

"Lily," I called.

She stopped walking and turned around. "Yeah?"

"Your bag is leaking," I told her.

Lily let out a yelp, threw her bag to the ground and opened it. It was then that the true horror was revealed.

"Oh my god!" screamed Lily, reaching into the bag and dragging out a massive handful of something disgusting. "What is this?"

I had no intention of getting close enough to find out. I took a quick step back. "Ah, go," I instructed. "Go and clean up."

"Charli did this, Miss," she declared. "I know she did."

Lily waved a fistful of the muck at me, sending chunks falling to the floor.

"Okay," I replied calmly. "I'll deal with it."

I had no choice but to. It was my job. Letting it slide and putting it down to a case of 'girls being girls' wasn't an option. As far as I was concerned, the girls at Pipers Cove High didn't behave like girls at all. They behaved like little animals.

Jasmine was a rabid dog. Lily was a turkey and Charli was the most venomous of spiders. Left alone, she was pretty to look at. When provoked, she became deadly.

We'd spent a lot of time together lately. Afternoon detention imprisoned both of us. We didn't usually speak but that afternoon curiosity got the better of me. I sat at my desk, rolling my pen between my fingers while I stared at her. "Charli, what did you put in Lily's bag?"

She leaned back in her chair, giving me the exact same look her brother did when he was about to say something cocky. "An open bottle of water and two loaves of bread," she replied. "I even cut the crusts off them."

"Don't you get tired?" I asked curiously. "Doesn't it wear you down?"

She shrugged. "I give as good as I get. If they ever decide to call a truce, I'll be happy to leave them alone."

I nodded, marginally placated. "Well, until then, you and I are going to be spending a lot of time together."

The prospect didn't seem to faze her in the least. "There are worse ways to kill an afternoon."

"You're a constant source of worry for your brother. You know that, don't you?"

Mentioning Alex wasn't smart. It immediately got her back up.

"What would you know about it?" she snapped. "You have no idea what Alex thinks."

I bit my tongue – very hard. I knew a lot of things about Alex, including what he thought of her continual need to rebel against the world.

"I'm merely pointing out that it can't be easy on him," I clarified. "You're constantly in trouble."

Charli glared at me for a painfully long time, probably waiting for me to back down and look away. I refused to so the stare-down continued.

"It's four o'clock," she said finally. "Can I go now?"

I nodded, still fighting the war of the cutting stares. "Yes. You may go."

I wasn't expecting to get the last word in so having her call out to me as she got to the door came as no surprise.

"Mademoiselle Décarie."

I twisted in my chair to look at her. "Yes?"

"Just so you know," she said, grinning slyly. "Alex gave me the bread."

10. VENGEANCE

I had to wait two more days before quizzing Alex about his role in bread-gate. He turned up at my door just after seven for our usual Friday night secret date, looking as scruffy and handsome as always.

I made the first move by grabbing a fistful of his shirt and pulling him forward. My lips easily found his and we somehow managed to hold the position as he walked us all the way through the to kitchen. It only ended once he gripped his hands on my waist and lifted me onto the counter.

"You're in a good mood," he noted, pushing forward to wedge himself between my legs.

"You put me there," I replied.

He leaned forward to whisper. "No, I put you on the kitchen bench." My heart started racing. "Now I'm trying to work out what I'm going to do with you."

"You're going to free me," I said putting my hand on his chest to keep him at bay.

"And why would I do that?" he asked tilting his head to the side. "I have you right where I want you."

I dropped my hand, paving the way for him to make a move, which he did at warp speed. We were suddenly a tangle of hands and mouths.

"Stay with me tonight?" I whispered.

He buried his head in my neck, breathing a little hard. "I can't," he replied. "Not tonight."

And therein lies the rub. Gorgeous, young Alex disappeared in an instant. Responsibility-laden Alex took his place. I pulled my shirt back in place and fussed with the buttons, trying to pull myself together.

Alex took a step back and ran his hands through his hair, doing nothing to tidy it up. He had bedroom hair. End of story.

"Don't be mad," he said quietly, following up with a too-sexy grin. "We were getting along so well."

"I am not mad."

I pushed him aside and jumped off the counter. Busying myself by checking the dinner in the oven was the only thing I could think of to hide the fact that I was hurt.

When I opened the oven and made a grab for the dish inside, Alex took the oven mitts from me and took over. He lifted the dish out and set it down on top of the stove. "Is there something going on here, Gabs?" he asked, turning back to face me.

"Of course not," I huffed. "I enjoy nothing more than cooking a grand meal for my boyfriend that no one knows about." I threw out my arms. "He's gorgeous and smart and incredibly good in bed. You know how I know he's good in bed?"

"No," he replied, daring to grin at my theatrics. "How?"

"Because that's where we end up – usually after dinner, sometimes before," I replied, dropping the choler and killing his smile. "And then he leaves me and goes back to whatever the hell he was doing before he came here and pretended to be mine for a while."

I'd made it sound like such a pathetic story. Anyone who didn't know better would think I was referring to another woman rather than a problematic teenage sister.

"I don't know what you expect me to do."

I could tell he was at a complete loss. He also looked worried. The next words out of my mouth did nothing to calm him. "I think you should tell Charli about us."

He was shaking his head before I'd even finished my sentence. "I don't think – "

"We've been together for months, Alex," I reminded. "You said you wanted to be sure we were going to work. We've held it together through everything. Why must we keep it a secret?"

His brown eyes bored into me while he nervously chewed his bottom lip. "Once it's out everyone will know. Gossip in this town is terrible. You've seen what she's been through."

"She'll handle it, Alex," I assured.

"It's not even Charli's issue, Gabs," he replied. "I've tried very hard to keep things constant for her. This is going to change everything."

I nudged him aside while I dealt with dinner. "She's not the impressionable little kid you seem to think she is," I insisted.

I felt qualified to say it because I'd spent almost as much time with her as he had lately, and I reminded him of it.

"Detention today?" He sounded surprised. "She never told me."

I took two plates out of the cupboard and set them down on the counter. "What were you expecting to happen after her little episode with Lily? By rights, you should've been sitting at the desk next to her."

Alex leaned his back against the counter and folded his arms. I quickly glanced across at him as

I threw open the drawer next to him. He looked completely perplexed.

"*Le pain*, Alex – the bread," I reminded, grabbing a serving spoon. "You gave it to her. That makes you an accomplice."

He was quiet for a long moment. I used the time to mutter under my breath about the horrid state of my overcooked fish dish.

"Gabrielle, what did she do with the bread?"

I stopped what I was doing to look at him. "You really don't know? She said you gave it to her."

His short explanation was laced with ire. Floss Davis has a pet Cape Barren goose called Kevin. The sister from hell had sweetly offered to stop in and feed it the two loaves of stale café bread Alex was planning to throw out that morning. Obviously, she'd found a better use for it.

"Floss has a goose called Kevin?" I asked, getting off subject.

"And a handful of cats," he replied. "Geoffrey is my favourite."

I giggled so hard that I had to put the spoon down on the bench. Alex didn't laugh. He was more interested in getting me back on subject.

"Tell me what she did with the bread," he demanded.

I quickly told him the story. "It was ugly," I said pulling a face. "Especially the way it squelched when Lily put her hand into the bag."

Alex furiously shook his head. "So what am I supposed to do with her?"

"Nothing," I replied.

"Just let it slide?" he asked doubtfully.

"Yes. Don't even mention it. It was an act of vengeance, not malice," I explained. "You must understand the difference."

I turned around, picked up our plates and made my way over to the dining table. Alex followed closely behind.

"Vengeance for what?"

I made sure he was seated before telling him. Even then, I hesitated.

"Lily wrote something crass on Charli's locker door," I revealed.

He practically growled out the question. "What was it?"

"Charlotte the harlot," I mumbled.

Alex's mouth formed a grim line. "And how did she know it was Lily?"

I smiled, figuring he was going to enjoy my answer. "A couple of reasons. It was written in bright pink lipstick and it was spelt wrong."

His shoulders dropped as he relaxed. I reached for his hand across the table. "She stands up for herself perfectly well, Alex," I assured. "Not always in the right way but believe me when I tell you that no one gets the better of her."

He nodded and looked down at the plate in front of him. "What kind of chicken stew is this?"

"It's fish."

He looked up at me, flashing me a cheeky smile. "Are you sure?"

"Shut up and eat your dinner," I grumbled. "Then you can take me to bed."

11. ART

Despite what I'd told him, Alex didn't let bread-gate slide. He locked everything that meant anything to Charli in the shed and grounded her. His only hope for survival after that involved getting out of the house.

He found sanctuary at mine, lazing around while we read the weekend papers. His lazy mood didn't last very long. Alex wasn't exactly renowned for sitting around doing nothing.

He dropped the folded newspaper down on the coffee table, stood up and walked over to my easel set up in the corner of the room. After a quick minute of studying the painting, he turned back to face me. "Where is this?"

"It's a place in France called Dieppe," I replied. "There's a grand old castle that sits high up on a cliff."

He restudied the half-finished painting. "You've been there?"

I walked over and stood beside him. "Not for a long time."

"And you remember this kind of detail?"

"Not all of it," I conceded. "I had to reference a few books."

"It's amazing, Gabs," he praised.

"It's no Claude Monet. His painting of the Dieppe cliffs was so good that it was stolen – twice."

Alex glanced across at me and smiled. "I think this is worth stealing. As soon as you're done, I'm going to swipe it, just so you'll know how good it is."

A small giggle escaped me. "Thank you. I'd be honoured to have you steal my work."

"Why aren't you painting a place you can see?" he asked curiously. "There are plenty of places around here worth painting."

"I know, but after a year of being here, I think I've covered the best ones."

He glanced at me as if I'd just sworn at him. "Impossible."

"It's true. I've painted the cliffs, the beach, the fields, the ocean, all of it."

Alex reached down and picked up and handful of brushes off the side table. "Pack you bags, sweetheart. We're going on a road trip."

I grinned widely, doing nothing to hide my excitement. "What do I need to take?"

"Paint, canvas and sensible shoes."

***

He wasn't kidding about the sensible shoes. If I'd known that our road trip would involve an hour of uphill hiking through a national park, I might have reconsidered agreeing to go.

"How much further?" I panted, trudging along behind him.

I really had no right to complain. Alex was the one carrying my bag of art supplies. All I had to carry was myself.

I'd decided against taking paint. My setup wasn't exactly mobile. If by chance we ended up somewhere inspirational, I'd draw it and paint it later.

"Be quiet and keep walking." Alex stopped walking for the hundredth time to let me catch up. "You wouldn't be so out of breath if you weren't using it all to complain."

"This place had better be magnificent, Alex," I grumbled.

He grinned back at me. "The harder the access, the sweeter the find, Gabs."

The access was definitely hard. I'd lost my bearings half an hour earlier when the bush became too thick to see through. I took heart in the fact that we still seemed to be walking along a fairly well worn trail and Alex didn't look scared or lost.

When we finally broke through to a clearing, I realised he was right. The find was sweet. From where we stood, we could see the whole town, and the ocean beyond it. I'd looked up at the massive hill behind the town many times. I'd even painted it – but I never imagined climbing it. Until today, I didn't even think it was possible. Even from a distance, the bush looked impenetrable. And we'd just conquered it.

"What do you think?" Alex asked, dumping my bag on the ground.

I kept my focus ahead. "I think I want to beat my chest and let out a triumphant cry."

He huffed out a quick laugh. "Settle down, Tarzan," he teased. "Paint me a picture instead."

I crouched down, unzipped my bag and took out the two sketchpads I'd packed. "We're drawing today. I'll share my pencils with you," I offered.

Alex shook his head. "I can't draw."

"And I couldn't swim," I retorted. But thanks to him, I'd finally learned. We'd been back to the black fairy lake many times. Once it got too cold to swim naked, Alex presented me with my very own wetsuit. It was bright pink and according to him, very unfashionable.

"Never wear it on a public beach," he warned me. "They'll slay you and I won't save you."

I didn't care. I thought it was fabulous. My swimming ability had become fabulous too. I was now an accomplished dogpaddler. Like my wetsuit, it wasn't sexy to look at but at least I could now save my own life if I ever fell into deep water.

I handed him a sketchpad and two pencils.

"Why two?" he asked naively.

"One is lighter than the other," I explained. "You might want to do some shading."

He huffed out a sharp laugh. "Stickmen don't need shading."

"Draw what you can see, Alex." I threw out my arms. "Look out there. You see the beauty in it, don't you?"

"Of course." He smiled. "That's why I brought you here."

I glanced around, trying to find somewhere to sit down. "Sit with me and draw it then."

"I am not sitting with you," he scoffed. "You might see that my drawing is far more awesome than yours, steal my ideas and go on to make a fortune."

I giggled at his silliness. "Fine. You sit there." I pointed to a large mossy rock behind him and walked a few metres away to claim my own. "I'll sit here."

Alex's eyes remained fixed on me while I sat down, flipped open my pad and began to draw. He finally followed suit, taking up position on the rock, sketchpad in hand.

"What am I supposed to draw?" he asked in a whiny voice I never usually heard from him.

"You have free run. It's art."

"And what is art, Gabs?"

I lowered my sketchpad and pointed to the view in front of us. "Art is beauty. Look out there and paint what you find beautiful."

"And wh- "

I cut him off. "Art is quiet too, Alex. Beautiful and quiet."

I saw him grinning at me from the corner of his eye. I fought hard not to smile too.

Unbelievably, he managed to keep quiet for the next half hour. I stole the occasional glance, surprised each time to see him actually drawing.

By the time I'd finished my picture, I was desperate to see his.

"Finished?" I asked.

"No," he huffed, feigning annoyance. "Be quiet and let me draw."

I gave him a few more minutes, but was soon at the point of exploding. I stood up and walked over to his rock. The second I reached him, he flipped his pad shut and stood up, holding it high out of my reach.

"Show me," I ordered.

He narrowed his eyes, holding his sketchpad against his chest. "Show me yours first."

I handed it to him.

"Do you even know how clever you are?" he asked, alternating glances between the picture in his hand and me.

I could feel the heat of embarrassment burning my cheeks. "Show me yours."

"Are you sure you want to see it? I don't want you to feel inferior."

I snatched the sketchpad from him so quickly that he nearly lost his grip on mine. I spun around out of his reach so I could check out his drawing.

He wasn't kidding when he mentioned stick figures. He'd drawn something that almost resembled a person – female I think. She had stick figure boobs. It had taken him forty-five minutes to draw stick figure boobs.

"Well?" he asked. "Don't leave me hanging."

I spun back to face him. "Is it a person?"

He dropped his head. "It's a woman. A beautiful coppery haired French woman," he explained theatrically. "If you'd given me coloured pencils, it would've been obvious."

I matched his laugh with one of my own. "Is it me?"

Alex stalked over to me and pulled the sketchbook from my grasp. He dropped both books down on the rock behind me and drew me in close. "You told me to draw something beautiful," he murmured against my mouth. "I don't think I did you justice."

I stretched up, linked my arms around his neck and kissed him with all I had. "I love you, Alex Blake," I declared, finally breaking free.

"Let's keep it real, sweetheart," he quipped. "You only love me for my art."

12. FLOWERS

I loved September in Australia, and there was no better place to be than my cottage. My little garden burst with colour. I'd lost count of the different kinds of flowers on display.

One of the great parts of having Alex for a boyfriend was the fact that he was very handy in the garden. He mowed my lawn, pruned trees and kept my woodheap stocked. Even greater, I got to watch him do it. There was no sexier sight than Alex Blake swinging an axe, especially when he'd been at it a while and had taken his shirt off. For my own selfish reasons, I always asked him to do it on a Friday afternoon. It was a ploy that benefited both of us.

He wasn't any help when identifying flowers, though. I picked a small purple flower, waved it at him and asked him what it was.

"I don't know, Gabs," he replied. "A purple flower?"

I smiled at him. "You are no help."

Alex took the flower from me and tucked it behind my ear. "I know someone who could tell you what most of these are."

I was delighted by the prospect. "Really?"

"Yeah." His handsome face twisted a little. "She's knowledgeable but difficult to deal with."

The demon child. Surely not!

"Is she also moody and easily aggravated?"

"That about sums her up."

I couldn't imagine Charli knowing a thing about flowers, but I was prepared to humour him. "Do you think she'll come here and tell me about them?"

He shrugged. "I can ask her."

I wasn't expecting to hear another word about it but Alex somehow got Charli to come through for me. Just an hour after leaving, he returned to the cottage, demon sister in tow.

I met them on the porch and the games began. Charli knew nothing of my relationship with Alex. As far as she probably knew, we weren't even friends.

Alex looked understandably nervous. His biggest mistake was not giving me the heads-up by cluing me in on the story he'd spun to get her there. I was flying blind.

"Ah, I explained to Charli that you needed some help identifying the flowers in your garden," he began. "We spoke about it the other day…. when you came into the café…. for coffee."

For a man who was determined to keep our relationship a secret, he was doing a terrible job of it. He was also pleading with me to save him by rapidly blinking his eyes.

I stepped off the porch and started walking toward the garden. "I'm so glad you remembered, Alex," I said casually. "I'd forgotten all about it."

Both Blakes followed me. Charli still hadn't spoken. I could feel Alex's panic because of it.

I turned back to face them. "I really appreciate this, Charli," I said sweetly.

Her shoulders moved as she shrugged. Her facial expression did not. "No big deal. What do you want to know?"

"Well," I picked one of the small purple flowers. "Do you know what this is?"

"You shouldn't pick them." Charli shook her head. "It's wasteful. Don't pick them without reason. If you leave them where they are, you'll get to enjoy them for longer."

Feeling suitably chastised, I cleared my throat. "Do you know what they are?"

"They're orchids," she replied.

I glanced at Alex, resisting the urge to roll my eyes. I knew what an orchid looked like. The flower I'd picked was small and spindly – nothing like an orchid. I held off on the eye rolling but something in my expression still gave me away.

"They're orchids, Mademoiselle," she repeated, less pleasantly than before. "They're native orchids." She began pointing out other flowers, none of which looked particularly similar. "And so are those and those and those. The one behind your ear is called a Caladenia, but it's still an orchid."

I made a quick grab for the flower tucked behind my ear, wondering what she'd say if she knew her brother had put it there.

Alex was must've been thinking the same thing. I glanced past Charli to him, immediately noticing that he was blushing. I'd never seen him blush before.

"These are called Clematis," continued Charli, pointing to a bush of tiny pink flowers at the edge of the rockery. "They can be pink, white or purple."

"Really?"

"Yes, really," she replied dully. "The Clematises belong here. They suit you." The look on her face was strange, as if she regretted saying it.

I couldn't help questioning her. "They suit me?"

"They signify mental beauty and art," she explained in a voice barely louder than a whisper.

I stole another glance at Alex. He wasn't blushing anymore. If anything, he looked as proud as punch.

The notoriously sullen girl managed to drop the demon act for the next fifteen minutes as we walked through the garden. I learned more than I could've learned in a whole season of researching it on my own.

Apparently, peonies signify shame and bashfulness. Daisies denote innocence and irises are what you send when you want to let someone know that you have a message for them.

"That is extraordinary, Charli," I truthfully praised. "How do you know this?"

She briefly turned back to Alex before answering. "It's just a hobby," she said humbly. "Alex once gave me a book about flowers."

He looked embarrassed again. I gave him the tiniest smile I could muster.

"Well, I think it's an amazing talent," I told her. "Do you have a favourite?" She pointed to the garden. "The tulips. They're important in any garden. You should probably plant more."

I turned to look at the sea of flowers behind me. The garden bed was full to the point of overflowing.

"I don't think I have any room."

"There's always room for more tulips, Mademoiselle," she replied.

It took all I had not to question Alex when I noticed him wink at her. I suddenly felt decidedly out of the loop but held my tongue. I'd probably pushed my luck to the limit where Charli was concerned. She'd been extremely helpful and borderline pleasant.

I thanked her instead – and Alex for no other reason than continuing with our stupid charade.

It was then that she floored me with a most unexpected offer. "You should come to our house some time soon," suggested Charli. "Our tulips are having a great run at the moment."

"Oh, I'd like that," I stammered.

She shrugged. "Cool."

Cool indeed. She'd unwittingly just given me permission to visit my boyfriend at his house for the very first time.

13. BELIEVING

I'd often wondered what Alex and Charli's house looked like. There was something remarkably sordid about the fact that I hadn't yet visited.

More than once I'd made Alex describe it to me. From what I knew, it was just a little bit bigger than the cottage and nowhere near as stylish. He'd seemed embarrassed when telling me that part but his demeanour soon changed when he explained how he'd spent two years bringing it back from ruin.

"It was a dump when I bought it," he told me. "Charli was only little. It was hopeless trying to get anything done while she was there. I probably could've had it finished a year earlier if she hadn't insisted on helping me paint."

I smiled at his reminiscing and then I felt a little sad. At an age when most young men are out living it up, he was renovating a house with a toddler so they'd keep a roof over their heads.

"How old were you?" I asked.

He shrugged. "I don't know. Twenty-one or two."

Stories like that made me want to never stop kissing him. It also made my mind spin in strange directions. I sometimes daydreamed, imagining a house full of kids with messy hair and cheeky smiles.

Reality usually dragged me back quite quickly. Considering I hadn't even visited his home yet, planning babies was probably jumping the gun.

***

I managed to hold off going out there for a whole day. On Sunday morning I texted Alex and asked for directions. It was ludicrous that I didn't know where he lived.

It took me fifteen minutes to get there. I would've made it in ten if I hadn't taken a wrong turn and ended up at the front gates of an alpaca farm. Until then, I hadn't even known there was an alpaca farm in Pipers Cove.

Eventually I bounced my small car up the rough gravel driveway and parked next to Alex's Ute. I felt like a nervous schoolgirl heading to a blind date. Having Alex meet me on the veranda put me at ease the tiniest bit. I wanted to lurch forward and kiss him, and then remembered I had a part to play.

I wasn't madly-in-love Gabs today. I was Mademoiselle Décarie who was supposed to be desperately keen to check out the tulip blooms.

I nervously smoothed down the back of my hair as I climbed the front steps.

"Relax, Gabs," beamed Alex. "Charli's not here."

I took a breath for the first time since getting out of the car. "Where is she? She was supposed to be here to show me the tulips."

He shrugged, still grinning. "She got a better offer. She's at Nicole's."

I was almost relieved to hear that irresponsible, thoughtless Charli was back in pole position. For some reason, she was easier to deal with than the marginally sweet version I'd met with a few days earlier.

Alex gripped my waist and drew me in close, kissing me intently. "I still want to see the tulips," I said, breaking free.

Keeping his hold on me, he straightened up and pointed down to the garden that sloped down the hill.

I blinked a few hundred times to make sure what I was looking at was real. I couldn't believe I'd missed it on the way up to the house. A gorgeous sea of red and orange blooms covered a huge area.

"You planted them?" I asked in disbelief.

Alex let out a low chuckle. "Every single one of them."

"Why so many?"

He tightened his hold and whispered in my ear. "Because fairies use them as beds for their babies."

I'd been with Alex for nearly six months. In that time, he'd regaled me with a handful of stories that I assumed he'd made up to suit the situation. It always struck me that they rarely had happy endings. One particular story about a fairy feeding her lover crushed glass to kill him as punishment for breaking her heart had nearly reduced me to tears.

I'd never known what to make of it. I just put it down to quirkiness. It was almost shocking to find that his younger sister was on the same wavelength. It made me wonder which of them was to blame for the nonsense.

"Who told you that?" I asked, twisting in his arms. "Where do these stories come from?"

He winked at me. "That'd be telling, wouldn't it?"

"That's the idea, Alex," I huffed. "I'm trying to work out if you're the crazy one or if it's all down to Charli."

"There's nothing wrong with believing in something, Gabs," he whispered.

"Do you believe?" I asked, still pressing for a straight answer.

He thought for a long moment, keeping his focus on my eyes the whole time. "I believe in giving little girls hope that magic is real. What's life without a little magic?"

"You told Charli these stories?"

He infinitesimally smiled. "For a long time, I had nothing else to give her."

***

My brother is four years older than me. We were close as children, grew apart as teenagers and closed the gap a little as adults. He now lives in Quebec with his wife. Both are attorneys, which seems to be a common career choice for Décarie men.

Obviously he'd had no hand in raising me, but he'd never felt the need to inject my life with moments of magic either. I couldn't deny it. I was struggling to understand the bond between Alex and Charli. I wasn't going to get any more information from him, so when he took my by the hand and led me inside, I vowed to use the opportunity to investigate some more.

He'd downplayed their quaint little house hugely. It was neat as a pin, nicely furnished and had a lovely homely feel.

I wandered to the centre of the lounge room, just as he'd done when checking out my cottage for the first time. "You made it out to be very different," I chided. "I was expecting beanbags and milk crates."

Alex dropped his head and smiled down at the floor. "Would you like a tour? I have an awesome bed."

Not that I'd ever admit it to him, I was very curious to check out his bedroom. But I also wanted to see the rest of the house. We'd already covered the lounge room. We moved on to the kitchen. And then we were done.

"That about covers it," he announced, walking us the very short distance to the lounge room.

"I love it," I told him. "Thank you for showing me around. You're a good host."

He smiled, and finally began to relax a little. "I'll make you some coffee."

"I'm actually trying to cut back on coffee," I revealed. "How about tea?"

He leaned down and chastely kissed me. "Coming right up."

Alex left the room, leaving me to check it out properly. The side wall was completely taken up by a long bookshelf. The Blakes obviously weren't readers. There was a tatty old copy of *Peter Pan*, an even tattier copy of *Robinson Crusoe* and a brand new French dictionary that looked as if it had never been opened. The irony was not lost on me.

I turned my attention to the assortment of photo frames. The pictures gave away no secrets. It looked like any other collection of family photographs. I noticed one of a woman, probably in her early thirties. I thought she vaguely resembled Charli and immediately jumped to the conclusion that it was their mother. Alex had hardly spoken of her, except to tell me she was a raging alcoholic who'd managed to drink herself to death at the tragically young age of forty.

Alex was the most private person I knew. It was hard not to take it personally. He never freely gave information and I tried hard not to push him. When he first told me that he loved me, I found the declaration extraordinary. I immediately questioned him about it.

"No big deal, Gabs. You love who you love," he reasoned. "The least I could do was tell you about it."

Those were the moments that reminded me why I endured such cloak and dagger. Bizarrely, it was also those moments that made me desperately want to understand him better.

One more thing on the shelf caught my eye. It was a Father's Day card. The word 'father' had been crossed out and replaced with Alex's name and a smiley face. In a wicked move, I took it off the shelf to read the inside.

This year I'm giving you 365 apologies. That's one for every day that

I was a jerk. Thank you for staying at the bottom of the tree.
Happy Alex Day!
Love and wishes,
Charli.

I suddenly had a huge lump in my throat that was impossible to swallow away. Before I had a chance to put it back, Alex appeared out of nowhere and said my name. I knew he was unhappy with me. He'd called me Gabrielle.

"I'm sorry," I stammered, quickly placing the card back on the shelf. "I don't mean to pry."

He set the mugs of tea down on the coffee table before speaking. "Yes you do," he said bleakly. "I haven't given you much to work with, have I?"

I hesitantly took a few steps toward him. "I'm trying so hard to build a life with you, Alex," I said in a plea for understanding. "You make it so difficult for us to move forward. I've tried hard to understand this situation but I just can't."

I literally watched the colour drain from his perfect face. "I'm going to tell you everything."

I rushed over to him and reached up, taking his face in my hands. "That's all I want."

His mouth fell open as if he was trying to speak but no sound came out. I waited for him to try again. "She's my daughter." His voice sounded nothing like his own. I was sure I'd misheard him.

I dropped my hold on his face and quickly shook my head, trying to shift the confusion from my brain. "Your what?"

"Charli is my daughter."

I felt my legs wobble. Alex must've noticed it because he grabbed my elbows and lowered me backward onto the couch. I couldn't think of a single thing to say and I barely heard a word of his rambling explanation.

I managed to pick up on a few key points. He'd had her at seventeen, her mother had never been a part of her life and his own mother had tried claiming Charli as her own. He hadn't even started the lie about being her brother. It was entirely his mother's doing.

"For the first time ever, I'd found a stable life in the Cove," he explained. "To make sure it was a *quiet*, stable life I kept up with the charade. I wanted Charli to grow up here."

The mention of her name brought an important question to the forefront – perhaps the most important one of all. "Does Charli know?" I choked.

His eyes drifted from mine and he slowly shook his head. "No. She has no idea."

I felt ill, so ill that I feared I might throw up. I jumped to my feet and made a beeline for the door.

"Stay, Gabrielle," he called. "Please."

I turned back to face him. "No. I can't do this. I'm so sorry."

I don't know if he spoke again. I ran to my car and didn't look back.

14. OFF TRACK

The next week moved impossibly slowly. Thankfully I'd given up coffee the week before. It made staying away from the café a little easier.

I hadn't heard a peep from Alex. I saw Charli almost every day. Of course, she was oblivious to the drama, just as she had been her whole life. I felt hugely sorry for the young girl. The last six months of my life had been a lie, but her whole life had been a lie.

It made me wonder how different she would be if she'd known the truth from the beginning, then realised it probably wouldn't have made a difference. At the end of the day Charli was just like any other sullen, moody sixteen-year-old girl. The notable difference between her and the rest of the pack was that she was smarter than most.

Stapling a girl to the pinup board by her hair is no mean feat.

I spent a total of four hours in detention with Charli that week, and it was more heinous than usual. I spent a lot of time staring at her, and trying not to be obvious about it.

Now that the truth was out, a million blanks had been filled. She was the spitting image of her father, which only added to my torture. I desperately wanted to ask her how he was, but couldn't think of a casual way of doing so.

I asked her about the process of stapling someone to a pinup board instead.

Charli smirked at me. "She volunteered."

I didn't believe her for a second. No girl in her right mind would voluntarily submit to that, even one as thick as Lily Tate.

***

I was looking forward to getting home. A good book, a glass of wine and my couch were calling me. As soon as I pulled onto the driveway, I realised a quiet evening was probably off the agenda.

Alex was there, chopping wood.

To say I was confused was an understatement. I spent a long few minutes sitting in my car, staring across the yard at him. It wasn't a manoeuvre that fazed Alex. His axe never missed a swing. Apart from one quick glance over his shoulder, he paid no attention to me.

Eventually, I got out of the car and wandered over to him. "Why are you here?" I punched out the question, sounding totally annoyed.

He swung hard and belted a log so hard that his axe got stuck. "I'm chopping your wood for you." He leaned down and wrenched his axe free. "You must be running low by now."

"Thank you," I muttered.

"No problem."

And that was that. He continued smashing wood and I stood there, doing nothing more productive than trying to stop the heels of my shoes sinking into the lawn.

"Are you coming inside?" I eventually asked.

"I'll bring some wood in for you," he said flatly.

"Thank you."

"No problem."

Ugh! The man was impossible. Alex Blake was in shutdown mode and I was certain I didn't deserve it. I'd done nothing wrong. I wasn't the one who lied. If anyone should've been pissed off, it was me.

"I shall take my own wood inside," I declared.

Alex dropped the axe to the ground and finally looked at me properly. "I shan't stop you," he mocked, infuriating me even more.

I'd gone too far to back down. I stooped down and picked up a small log, managing to keep a grip on it with one hand as I held it away from my body. It was a stupid display that made Alex laugh.

"It's going to take a long time if you're going to do it one pissy piece of kindling at a time," he teased. "Put a bit of back into it."

"I will manage," I grumbled, dropping the log and brushing my hands off.

"Put your arms out like this," he ordered, holding arms out and putting his elbows to his chest.

For reasons unknown, I mimicked him.

"Good girl," he said, right before he loaded my arms up with two heavy logs. "Now you're good to go."

Go where? The only place I was likely to go was flat on my face in a heap. My high heels had sunken into the lawn, pinning me to the ground. As hard as I tried, I couldn't even kick them off. I was stuck.

With no other option, I dumped the wood on the ground, sorted out my mobility issues and stormed into the house.

Alex strolled in a few minutes later, armed with enough wood to see me through the whole weekend. He stacked it neatly, arranged a few logs in the fireplace and spent the next few minutes getting it alight – all without saying a single word. It was excruciatingly obvious that he wasn't going to be the one to back down.

I blew out a long breath as I ventured into the room, clueless as to how it was going to play out.

"You don't need to do this," I said, holding my position behind the couch.

Alex stood up and dusted off his hands. "I don't mind."

"Will you stay for a while?"

He gazed at me for a long time before finally speaking. "No. I have to get home."

I nodded, pretending to understand. "Okay, well, you should go then."

He walked over to me, leaned down and planted a long kiss on my forehead. And then he was gone. He slipped out the door without saying another word.

15. RESOLUTION

I thought the strange shift between us would be temporary. Eventually we'd have to talk about things. We loved each other. People who love each other work to solve their problems.

At first, Alex's unwillingness to resolve anything with me was hard to comprehend, but then I realised he'd taken the hard line of believing that all the problems he had were his own.

I was completely on the outer. All my information came from studying Charli. I could usually tell when she and Alex were at loggerheads. She'd quieten down and pull her head in for a few days. When things were good at home, she was stapling people to pinup boards at school.

Alex and I rarely spoke. Awkward exchanges at the café were horrible. He'd make pointless small talk and we'd discuss the weather. I missed the flirty side of him. I missed everything about him – even the way he called me Gabs.

One thing didn't change. Bizarrely, he turned up at my cottage every Friday to chop wood. I didn't question it. I just accepted it because it meant that for a few short hours a week I could pretend he was still mine.

It would start with an hour of smashing wood and end with a kiss on my forehead. Sometimes he'd break the routine and tell me he missed me. I'd ask him to stay. He'd leave anyway. It was maddening.

It was a routine that had carried on for over six weeks.

Getting us back on track seemed impossible. I could barely recall what the track looked like, but remembered it being far more enjoyable than watching him stack wood and walk out the door.

As a last ditch effort, I took a chance and cooked his favourite meal, coq au vin. By the time he walked into the house that evening, the smell was wafting through the whole house.

I waited until he got the fire lit and then made my move. "I made you chicken for dinner."

Abandoning the fire, he turned to face me. "Thank you, but I can't stay."

"I'm not asking you stay," I shot back. "You can take it home with you. I figure it's the least I can do considering you've been keeping my fire going all these weeks. Consider it payment for services rendered."

His eyes left mine as he dropped his head and smirked down at the floor. "I've never been paid with chicken stew before."

I felt my whole chest tighten at the mere mention of stew. I wanted to run across the room and smack him.

"I remembered that it's your favourite," I said sourly. "I thought you'd like it."

He looked up at me again, smiling this time. "What are you planning to have for dinner?"

"Excuse me?"

"Well, if you're giving me the stew, what are you going to have?"

I shook my head a few times, unable to answer his silly question.

Alex stalked toward me, stopping when I was just about in reach. "To be fair, I should probably share the stew with you," he murmured, inching closer to me.

My heart was belting through my chest and breathing had suddenly become something that required effort.

"What's the matter, Gabs?" he asked in a deliciously low tone. "You seem a little flustered."

"You know exactly what you're doing, Alex," I whispered. "This is make or break time for you."

He leaned in, breathing his next words into my hair. "How do you figure that?"

"To be left hanging would be a cruel and unusual punishment," I said, sounding a little stronger. "Don't do it to me."

He put his hands on my shoulders and spun me around to face him, managing to kill the mood in an instant.

"Is that what you think?" he asked, aghast. "That I'm punishing you? You ended it, Gabrielle."

"I did no such thing!"

He dropped his hold on me and took a step back. A look of pure confusion swamped him. "If I remember correctly, your parting words when you left my house were along the lines of 'I'm sorry. I can't do this.' That sounded pretty final."

"I wanted to work it out," I said roughly.

He shook his head, frowning. "What do you want to work out? You can't handle my situation. I'm still living my situation. Nothing has changed."

"So you still haven't told her?" My voice was small.

"No, I haven't told her," he spat. "And I don't need a pushy princess dictating how the future with my kid is going to play out."

"What are you so afraid of, Alex?" I asked bravely.

The anger that was building quickly receded. He answered me calmly and painfully truthfully.

"She'll hate me, Gabrielle. I'm all she's ever known, and it's all been a lie. I'm protecting myself, not her."

I slowly shook my head. "She's going to have to know eventually."

"And I will cross that bridge when I come to it," he mumbled.

"And what about us?" I asked.

He finally smiled, and it was perfect. "I like us."

"I miss us," I replied.

Alex reached out and drew me in close. "You're my art, Gabs," he murmured.

I clung to his forearms, ensuring he kept a safe distance from me. I hadn't finished with him yet.

"What do you mean?"

He lightly pressed his warm lips to mine. "You told me that art is beauty. You're my beauty and I love you."

"Let's keep it real, sweetheart," I quipped. "You only love me for my stews."

16. VISITOR

Being back on track was spectacular. Being with Alex never grew old and I treasured every minute we spent together. Keeping our relationship to ourselves wasn't turning out to be so bad either. Our lives moved slowly, but we were still moving forward.

The school year finally ended and after a lovely warm summer, drifted into a new one. I expected Charli's final year of high school to be a little more laid back. Jasmine Tate finally graduated, leaving Lily and Lisa to do her bidding. Even combined they were no match for Charli. By the end of the first term, they'd all but given up on their campaign to destroy her. Nasty comments between the two factions were inevitable, but nothing compared to the year before.

That meant I got a reprieve too. I hadn't spent time holed up with Charli in detention for months. I almost missed her.

Alex wasn't missing the demon version of his secret daughter one bit. Slowly but surely he was making plans to tell her the news he'd been keeping from her since she was born.

Charli had big plans of travelling at the end of the school year. He knew that would be his cut off point. She'd leave town knowing that she wasn't freeing up her brother to finally live his own life. She'd be leaving her father, and he was going to miss her dreadfully.

***

I wasn't looking forward to telling Alex my news, which was strange because I was truly excited. There was no point trying to ease into it, but I tried softening the blow by picking my moment well.

We were in bed when I hit him with it. I laid my cheek on his warm chest as if that was all it would take to keep him from bolting out of my bed.

My cousin had plans to visit, which meant our Friday rendezvous' would be put on hold for as long as he was in town.

"How long is he planning to stay?" asked Alex sounding bitterly disappointed.

"A couple of months," I muttered unwillingly.

Alex let out a long sigh that I felt beneath my cheek. "So where does that leave us?"

I ran my fingertips lightly down the ridges of his chest. "We'll work it out."

"When is he coming?"

"He'll be here tomorrow."

Alex's shifted, giving me no choice but to move. I sat up, taking most of the sheet with me. "I didn't know he was coming," I explained. "He was supposed to be going to Spain. I'm not sure what the story is, but his plans have fallen through."

Alex reached up and put his hand behind my neck. He stared at me for a long moment while he thought it through. "It's not the end of the world, I suppose," he finally grumbled. "I'll just have to be more creative when it comes to – "

I put my finger to his lips. "Don't dare finish that sentence," I warned. "You're in the company of a lady."

He pulled me down onto the bed and swiftly rolled on top of me. "I've heard you talk dirty, Gabs," he teased, making me giggle. "You're no lady."

***

Adam Décarie is my favourite cousin, despite the fact that I am six years older than him. When he was little, I used to pretend he was mine. My eight-year-old brain saw nothing wrong with mothering a little two-year-old.

As we grew, I found that I still tended to mother him. I was worried about seeing him for the simple fact that he sounded out of sorts when he'd called to let me know he was on his way. I got the impression there was a reason Adam was headed to Pipers Cove.

My offer to collect him from the airport had fallen on deaf ears. He'd arranged a car and was making the hour long journey by himself. Adding to my worry was the fact that it had been pelting down with rain all day and he was unfamiliar with driving on the left hand side of the road.

When he finally arrived, I breathed a sigh of relief, thankful I wasn't going to have to phone my aunt with terrible news. Tante Fiona wasn't the easiest of women to deal with.

I met Adam on the porch. He greeted me with a wide smile and lifted me off my feet as he hugged me tightly.

"Put me down," I ordered. "You're soaked."

He lowered me to my feet and I pushed him away to get a better look at him. He was such a lovely looking man, the epitome of tall dark and handsome. He also happened to be soaked to the bone.

"Why are you all wet?" I asked curiously.

He grinned widely, ignoring the beads of water dripping off his dark hair onto his face. "I nearly killed a girl, Gabi."

I wondered for a moment if my English had failed me. I asked him to repeat his words in French.

"She was gorgeous," he told me, still smiling. "Blonde and angry and seriously uptight."

My heart sunk. I knew only one girl who fit the bill. "What was her name?"

He shook his head. "I don't know, she didn't tell me."

"Oh, well," I crowed, trying to downplay it. "No harm done."

I was microscopically hopeful that that would be the end of it. All I had to do was keep him away from Charli for the next two months. I wasn't expecting it to be a difficult task. I could think of nothing they'd have in common.

I hooked my arm through his and led him toward the door. "Come inside. You can get dry and tell me all your news. I'll cook us a nice dinner."

"Ah, don't go to any trouble for me, Gabi," he said sheepishly.

I released my hold on him. "It's no trouble."

Adam pulled a strange face as he worked hard to let me down gently. "I've actually made plans."

"What plans?" I snapped. "You've only been in town ten minutes."

He laughed and dropped his head. "I'm going to a wedding."

"Joanna Lawson's wedding?"

Adam shrugged. "I don't know whose wedding it is. All I know is that the angry blonde is going to be there."

"So?" I barked, horrified.

"So, there's something about her. I can't explain it."

If he had ten thousand years of knowing Charli Blake he'd be none the wiser. She was impossible.

***

The only good to come of Adam disappearing out the door on his first night in town was that it meant Alex could come over.

I practically rushed him at the door. I grabbed his hand and pulled him over to the couch. "We need to talk," I demanded.

"Why?" he asked, perplexed. "What have I done?"

I quickly rushed through the very short story of Adam and Charli.

Alex mulled it over for a long time before finally speaking. "I'm not sure why you're so worried, Gabs. She hasn't caused anyone bodily harm in a long time. He'll be fine."

I wiped the smug grin off his face in the best way I knew how – I pointed out the worst-case scenario. "How are you going to cope if this progresses?"

"Into what?" he asked, looking slightly worried.

I hammed it up, spelling it out to him in my best theatrical voice. "Two young lovers from completely different walks of life – thrown together by a chance meeting during a rainstorm."

He pulled me backward into the cushion of the couch, pressing his lips against mine. "Stop talking," he murmured against my mouth.

I momentarily broke free and continued with the Broadway-style voice. "Were they destined to meet? Will their love survive? Will – "

"Will. You. Shut. Up."

I dropped my head, giggling against his neck. "This might be trouble, Alex," I warned.

THE END